Just Grace
Walks the Dog

Just Grace Walks the Dog

Written and illustrated
by
Charise Mericle Harper

Houghton Mifflin Company

Boston 2008

The text of this book is set in Dante MT.
The illustrations are pen and ink drawings digitally colored in Photoshop.

Library of Congress Cataloging-in-Publication Data
Harper, Charise Mericle.
Just Grace walks the dog / written and illustrated by Charise Mericle Harper.
p. cm.
Summary: Eight-year-old Just Grace and her best friend Mimi embark
on a campaign to convince Grace's parents that they are
responsible and dependable enough to get a dog.
ISBN-13: 978-0-618-95973-0
[1. Dogs—Fiction. 2. Responsibility—Fiction.
3. Schools—Fiction. 4. Diaries—Fiction.] I. Title.
PZ7.H231323Jw 2008
[Fic]—dc22
2007041169

For the great
dogs I have loved

Mika and Emma

UNFORTUNATE THINGS

There are two kinds of unfortunate things: those that are unfortunate because they have not happened, and those that are unfortunate because they already really did happen. I am pretty unlucky, because right now in my life I have both kinds of unfortunate things happening at the exact same time! My unfortunate thing that did not happen is that I am not allowed to have a dog, and my unfortunate thing that did happen is that at school everyone calls me Just Grace.

Some people say that when bad stuff happens in your life it gives you lots of character, which means that you end up being a super-interesting person when you grow up. I must be filling up with character pretty fast, because unfortunate stuff is always especially happening to me. Maybe that means I'll be on TV or something when I get big.

UNFORTUNATE ON PURPOSE AND UNFORTUNATE MISTAKE

When something unfortunate happens it is probably better if the unfortunate thing is a mistake instead of an on-purpose unfortunate thing. So I am at least lucky about that, because my biggest unfortunate thing was definitely 100 percent an accident.

**UNFORTUNATE
ON-PURPOSE THING**

**UNFORTUNATE
MISTAKE THING**

MY UNFORTUNATE THING

My real name is Grace, but at school my name is Just Grace, which is an unusual, stupid, and completely dumb name. How something can change from nothing special to completely dumb is a long, unfortunate story, and one that I am very tired of explaining. But if I don't explain it, then people think that it's an on-purpose thing and that my parents were crazy to name me that, and that I have been living with the awful Just Grace name since the day I was born, and maybe even worse, that I actually like it. And then they will look at me like I am 100 percent Just Grace. So I have to tell them the story so they can know that only my outside is Just Grace and that on my insides I'm a solid Grace all the way through. It's like being a girl M&M. I look like Just Grace/candy on the outside, but on the inside I'm all Grace/chocolate! It might not seem like it, but it makes a big difference!

JUST GRACE OUTSIDE

CANDY OUTSIDE

CHOCOLATE INSIDE

GRACE INSIDE

CANDY M&M   **GIRL M&M**

HOW THIS UNFORTUNATE THING HAPPENED

There are four girls named Grace in my class. Miss Lois, my teacher, said that we all had to change our names or she would never be able to get the right Grace's attention when she said "Grace." Even when she was explaining this I could kind of tell she was right because all four of us looked up when she said Grace, and Peter Marchelli, who sits right next to me, didn't even stop doodling on his desk. Miss Lois named Grace Wallace "Grace W.," and Grace Francis "Grace F.," and Grace Landowski "Gracie," and then right before she got to me I said, "Well, if everyone else is having a new name, can I be called just Grace?" Since no one else was using the

Grace name, it seemed like maybe I could have it. But Miss Lois didn't understand me, and even when I tried to tell her about her mistake she still didn't listen, or even care about it anymore. She closed her ears and wrote Just Grace in her rule book of class names and attendance.

ONCE SOMETHING IS WRITTEN IN THIS BOOK IT CAN NEVER BE CHANGED, EVEN IF IT IS WRITTEN IN PENCIL!

And then suddenly it was school law forever, that my new dumb name was Just Grace, because once it is written in the book it can never be changed.

The first person to make fun of me was Grace F., and that was no surprise because back then she was still the Big Meanie and I thought she hated me.

But that was before she changed back into Grace F., who is really very funny and an excellent artist, which are two things you would not imagine could be true until you got to know her.

THREE GRACES PLUS ONE

Grace F., Grace W., and I all had to do a project together, and that is how we all became friends. Grace L. was in another group so she got to be friends with Walker Marcie and Bethany, but I still think it made her sad that she was not friends with us, because our names were all Grace and she was a Grace too, but not one who was in our group. I can figure out stuff like that because of my teeny tiny superpower. My superpower helps me know when people are unhappy, even if they are pretending to be happy, and even if they are very good actors. It's called empathy power. The hard thing about superpowers is that they don't come with an instruction book so it's not always easy to know exactly when and how to use them. I think other superpowers, like

SUPERSTRENGTH POWER—EASY

EMPATHY POWER—NOT EASY

superstrength or x-ray eyes, would be a lot easier to work.

I felt sorry for Grace L. when we other Graces were joking around and having so much fun calling each other Grace, Grace, and Grace. But I couldn't figure out what to do to help her, so I pretended I didn't notice she was sad. This is a very hard thing for a person with my superpower to do, and it can sometimes end up giving me a stomachache.

IF I IGNORE MY SUPERPOWER, I FEEL SICK FOR A LITTLE WHILE.

MR. FRANK

Today was the last day I will ever see Mr. Frank standing in my classroom at school. He was our student teacher and the real reason I became friends with Grace W. and Grace F., who used to be the Big Meanie. He made me work with them when we had to do a language project. Sometimes when someone forces you to do something you would not normally do, the ending part and how it works out is a surprise, one that you would have never guessed in a million years. I would have never thought that I would be friends with or even like the Big Meanie. But I was lucky, because this forcing thing only sometimes works out in a good way.

Dad had to work on a project with a man named Jeremy at his job, and now he says he doesn't like the Jeremy man very much anymore. Before Dad knew him better he thought Jeremy was funny and a hard worker, but now he says Jeremy takes too many coffee breaks and is irresponsible, which is a word I was happy he was using about someone else and not me.

Anytime I do something wrong Dad loves to use the *irresponsible* word on me, and usually he likes to use it more than once or twice in a row.

IRRESPONSIBLE EXAMPLE

IT IS IRRESPONSIBLE TO LEAVE JAM OUTSIDE ON THE PICNIC TABLE BECAUSE IT WILL SOON BE FILLED UP WITH ANTS AND THEN WE WILL HAVE TO THROW IT IN THE GARBAGE.

THREE NEW THINGS

It was not hard to say goodbye to Mr. Frank. I did not cry like Jane Dublin did. She will probably never see him again, so I can understand why she was so sad she had to cry. He has to go back to the university to finish off all his learning before he can get his certificate that says he is a real teacher. Before he came to our school I didn't know it took so much work just to stand in front of our class and tell us what to do. The real reason I did not cry or feel bad about Mr. Frank leaving is that Grace F. lives right next door to him. She says I can come over to her house anytime I want to see Mr. Frank. And even though her mom won't let us knock on his door, because that would be bothering him, we can probably still see him because she says he usually comes outside if he hears you talking to his dog through the fence. He has a very fat and very friendly golden retriever named Winkie.

I am definitely going to visit Grace F., because one visit to her house will give me three new things all at the same time. I will get to see her bedroom, I will get to call Mr. Frank "Jeffrey," the way she does when he is not in school, and I will get to play with Winkie, his golden retriever. I am newly crazy about dogs. They are like cats, which I already liked, but better because you can take them places with you like a real friend. Plus you can teach them to do tricks and they will try to learn them, which cats definitely don't do.

MIMI

Mimi is my best friend in the whole world and she lives right next door to me. This is extra lucky because stuff like that hardly ever happens. The even better part is that we can see each other from our bedroom windows. Mimi got a book from the library so we could learn Morse code and send flashlight messages to each other at night in the dark. We have tried to do it a couple of times but it's kind of hard and it takes a really long time. I think it's much easier to send the message to Mimi than to figure out the message that she is sending to me. Still, it's a good idea, and if we keep practicing we might get really good at it. It would be excellent to stay up all night flashlight talking. And the extra best part is that none of our parents would ever even know about it.

COVER OF MORSE CODE BOOK

HOW TO DO FLASHLIGHT MORSE CODE

Flashlight Morse code is not fun and easy like it said it was going to be on the cover of Mimi's book. Flashlight Morse code is confusing and frustrating, but they couldn't put that on the cover because then no one would try it. Every letter of the alphabet has a different code, and it's all dots and lines. You have to spell out everything you want to say letter by letter using the right code. A dot means you flash the flashlight on and off really fast, and a dash means you leave the flashlight on for longer. Just to spell out "hi" you have to do four fast flashes for the *h* and then two fast flashes for the *i*. Mimi and I both copied out the code chart and taped it to our windows, but it's still not easy to do. Mimi said the easy part was a lie, but she was sure the fun part would be true if we practiced more.

MORSE CODE CHART

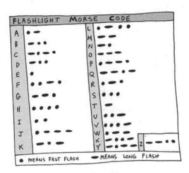

MIMI AND CATS

Mimi is allergic to cats, which is why they used to be my favorite animal and why they are not now. Mrs. Luther, my other next-door neighbor, has a great cat named Crinkles. She says he is a cat-dog, which means she thinks he is kind of like an M&M

too, cat coating on the outside and mostly dog on the inside. I don't think she is really right about that, though. I have tried to teach Crinkles some really easy tricks, and he did not even try to do them at all. If he was part dog, he would love to learn new stuff. Every time I touch Crinkles I have to remember to wash my hands and change my clothes before I see Mimi, or else she will start her sneezing. So it is much easier to just not touch him instead. Mimi is worth it.

MIMI AND DOGS

I thought I would forever not have an animal friend in my life until Mimi said that she thought she might not be allergic to dogs. She went to visit her uncle, and his new dog, Chesapeake, did not make her sneeze even once. And even though she didn't touch him, this was a big surprise, because if she even stands next to a cat she will sneeze like crazy and then have to take her medicine so her eyes don't get puffed up like supersize marshmallows.

SO PUFFY SHE CAN HARDLY OPEN THEM.

SHE SAYS THEY ARE SUPER ITCHY TOO!

MIMI WITH NORMAL EYES

MIMI WITH PUFFED-UP EYES

Mimi is also not allergic to frogs, lizards, snakes, turtles, birds, and fish, but those are not animals that I would want for a pet. I like animals with fur who are cuddly and can make you feel better just by hugging them.

I asked Mom and Dad if I could have a dog and they said no and that to have a dog you have to be dependable and responsible. *Responsible* is the opposite of *irresponsible,* so it is no surprise that Dad thought of that part. *Responsible* and *dependable* are a lot alike, so I made up a chart to show how a good pet owner like me would behave to be both. And then so Mom and Dad could know that I was being serious, I taped it to the fridge. We have one of those fridges that look magnetic but then when you put a magnet on them the magnet just falls off. That means we have to tape everything on, which is much uglier, plus we don't get to use cute or funny magnets like most other people do.

DEPENDABLE	RESPONSIBLE
- FEED DOG 2 TIMES A DAY. - TAKE DOG OUT FOR WALKS EVERY DAY. - BRUSH DOGS FUR. - GIVE DOG WATER SO HE DOES NOT DRINK OUT OF THE TOILET. - LOVE DOG EVERY DAY.	- COME HOME RIGHT AFTER SCHOOL TO LET DOG OUT. - MAKE SURE DOG'S FEET ARE NOT MUDDY. - DO NOT LET DOG EAT GARBAGE. - TAKE DOG TO THE DOCTOR IF HE IS SICK.

MIMI TEST

Mimi and I decided to go to the park to test for sure that she is not allergic to dogs. There are always dogs in the park, so it was easy. We stayed for over an hour and played with three little dogs and two big dogs, and

Mimi did not even have one single sneeze the whole time. It was amazing! She even let one of the dogs lick her chin. I was worried about that because that was awful close to her eyes, and you really aren't supposed to let strange dogs lick your face. I think she was just so excited to be close to a friendly, furry animal that she couldn't help it. It was hard to get Mimi to leave since she has been starved of animal attention her whole entire life. When something super good is happening, it is hard to give it up and just go home. We talked all the way home about how we

MIMI WITH REAL DOG

couldn't believe all the time we had wasted when we could have had a dog in our lives. And how that was going to have to change really soon.

ANIMAL PEOPLE

Mimi is not allowed to have a dog because her parents are not animal people. Her mom and dad did not have any pets when they were growing up, so they can't really help the way they are. It is very hard to change a non–animal person into an animal person. My mom and dad both had pets when they were kids so they have to be animal people, even though when I asked them they said they are not. They probably wouldn't admit it but they are sort of like M&M's too. They have non–animal person outsides with animal person insides. All I have to do is peel off their outside non–animal person shells.

MOM AND DAD

SHELL ON   **SHELL OFF**

DOG CHOICES

Mimi says that she is more of a big-dog person than a little-dog person. I don't know how she can know that, because up until we went to the park she didn't know if she was even an any-kind-of-dog person. At first I thought it was maybe because little dogs reminded her of cats and her allergies, but she said it wasn't that. Now I think it's because she is so excited about dogs that she wants to have as much dog as she can get. It's like if you suddenly tasted ice cream for the first time in your life and found out you totally loved it. You'd want to eat the whole container. I told Mimi that I think our chances of being allowed to have a dog are better if we pick a little dog, because a little dog is closer to a no dog than a big dog is.

NO DOG   CAT-SIZE DOG   VERY SMALL DOG   SMALL DOG   MEDIUM DOG   BIG DOG

MAX

Max is Mimi's next-door neighbor. He is my one-house-away neighbor. He and Mimi and Sammy Stringer did their school project together, which is how they all became friends. Sammy spends a lot of time visiting with Max. Sometimes Mimi and I do stuff with them, because if they are right there standing outside it's not polite to ignore them.

Sammy is not my favorite person, but I am starting to like him a little better. Mom says your tastes change when you grow up, so I guess that is what's happening. So far I still don't like grapefruits or cabbage or peas or spinach, so the food-tastes-changing part probably hasn't started yet. When Mom was little she said she didn't like potatoes or tomatoes, but now that she is grown up she loves them. I hope she is wrong about the food-tastes-changing part, because I can't imagine

eating a cabbage and saying "yummy" at the same time. That would be disgusting!

PICKING A DOG

Max came over when Mimi and I were standing outside talking about the kinds of dogs we liked. "German shepherds are the best dogs ever," said Max. "My uncle has one, and Lady can do all sorts of tricks and even lets you use her tummy as a pillow when you want to take a nap." "Oh my gosh! That sounds perfect!" said Mimi. "I think we should get a German shepherd!" "Wow! Are you getting a dog?" asked Max. "I could teach it some tricks." Talking to Max was not helping Mimi to change her mind and forget about picking a big dog. So I said, "Isn't a German shepherd the same kind of dog that Mr. Hurley has?" Mr. Hurley is our neighbor across the street, and his dog, Oliver, who is a German shepherd, is not even a teeny tiny one bit friendly. He acts like he can't wait to get away from you, and Mr. Hurley always says, "Leave him be, children. He's not used to you little ones." Even though none of us is really that little anymore.

"Yeah, well, that's because he's seventy-seven years old," said Max. "Mr. Hurley is that old?" I was surprised. Mr. Hurley looked old, but old like my dad, not old like a grandpa. "No, not him, silly—Oliver." Now Max was laughing at me. "Oliver is seventy-seven dog years old, which is eleven years old in human years." Sometimes Max thinks he is such a smarty-pants and the knower of everything about everything. I was glad when Mimi said, "I don't know—Oliver doesn't seem like he was ever very friendly. And his fur doesn't look very soft either." We would have probably talked about it some more, but Sammy walked up and Sammy is not a furry-animal person. Not on the outside or on the inside.

RESPONSIBLE AND DEPENDABLE

Mom and Dad said that it takes much more than making a list to prove that you are responsible and dependable. Then they told me all the kinds of things that dog owners have to do. I knew about most of them already, but not the part about having to clip the dog's toenails. It sounded kind of gross and hard to do, but I pretended I already knew all about it. Of course Dad also talked about having to pick up the poop. Nobody likes that part, but I bet if I wore rubber gloves and didn't breathe through my nose I could do it. It's the only really yucky thing about having a dog.

Then, while my brain was still thinking about everything, Dad said, "Maybe we can talk about it again when you are older." He always says this when I ask about something fun that he doesn't want me to have. When I'm older I'm going to be so busy with all the fun things I don't get to do now that I won't even have time to do my homework, and it will be all his fault!

I went up to my room to be mad all alone and draw a comic. Sometimes when I am feeling bad it helps me if I draw something.

MISS LOIS

Miss Lois is my teacher at school, and I used to not really like her very much, but that was mostly because I didn't understand her yet. It's like the thing that happened with liking the Big Meanie better, only Miss Lois is a grownup and she never stuck her tongue out at me. Now that Mr. Frank is gone, Miss Lois is going to be our only teacher again. I didn't even try to ask her about changing my Just Grace name, because she would have for sure said no. In Miss Lois's head, right next to her great love of elephants, because that is her favorite animal, is my Just Grace name. And just like an elephant, she is never going to forget it. Elephants are supposed to have amazing memories, so that is too bad for me.

MISS LOIS THINKING

MISS LOIS'S NEW PROJECT

Miss Lois wants us all to keep a journal and to write in it every day for a whole week. She gave everyone in the class a special red notebook to use for the project. She said she is not going to share what we write with the rest of the class, so we can write about stuff that is sort of private if we want to, but that we should remember that *she* is going to read it to make sure we did everything like we were supposed to. I guess she doesn't want us to be embarrassed about what we write down.

Miss Lois said it's easy to keep a journal if you pick the same time to work on it each day. That way you won't forget about writing in it and miss days, and then have to make up a bunch of stuff at the last minute before you have to hand it in. She also said we could use drawings and photos if we wanted, which is great, because I love to make both of those things. Before I knew Miss Lois better I didn't think she liked pictures, so it was a big happy surprise to find out that she likes to draw. We have to write at least four sentences every day, and they can't be the same four sentences over and over. I know that because Drake Brooks said, "I eat waffles for breakfast every morning—can I just write that each day?"

EVERYONE HAD TO WRITE THEIR NAME HERE. OF COURSE I HAD TO WRITE JUST GRACE

THE RED NOTEBOOK

WHAT IS GOOD ABOUT WRITING IN A JOURNAL

Miss Lois said that writing in a journal every day is rewarding and it shows commitment. The rewarding part is that when you get older you can look back and see what you were thinking and doing when you were young, because she said we are all going to do lots of forgetting as we get older and we won't remember everything we are doing right now. The commitment part shows that you are dedicated and dependable.

As soon as Miss Lois said *dependable* it made me a lot more excited about the project. When I was finished I was going to show it to Dad and he would have to cross the dependable part off of my list of stuff I have to prove to him. Then all I would have to do was find something for the responsible part. I couldn't wait to tell Mimi we were closer to a dog already.

After school Mimi and I did some more dog talking, and even though we are both excited about dogs, we are not excited about the same dog. Mimi is not giving up on her love for a big dog, and I am not giving up on my love for a little dog. This means we have a big problem. Being best friends does not always mean you like the same things every single time. Sometimes it would be 100 percent easier if this was true.

BIG DOG VERSUS LITTLE DOG

THE BEST SHOW IN THE WORLD

Instead of fighting about dogs, we decided to go and watch an episode of *Unlikely Heroes*. This is our most favorite show in the whole world. Every week they show you different real normal people who have done super-hero-type things.

Last week there was a man who jumped in front of a car to save a runaway baby stroller from getting hit. The car hit the man and he went flying over the top of it and landed right on the roof of the car behind. Except for a sprained finger, he wasn't even hurt. This was a good thing, because there wasn't a baby in the stroller and if the man had been hurt for nothing that would have been really sad. Everybody at the accident said the man was a hero anyway, and I guess that made him happy because he was smiling a lot when the show's hosts were interviewing him.

Max came outside just as we were walking up Mimi's steps, so we asked him if he wanted to watch the show with us. Max loves *Unlikely Heroes* too, but that is only because we told him so much about it. Before he moved next door to Mimi he hadn't even really watched it.

HOW TO SOLVE A PROBLEM

Before the show started Mimi and I had to argue about big dogs and little dogs a little more—we couldn't help it. It surprised me

100 percent, but Max came up with a way so that we would never fight about dogs again. He said we should make a chart of all the dogs we met and write down everything that was good and bad about each one. Then at the end we could go down the list and pick the best dog. It was such a perfect way for us to decide on our dog. I couldn't believe that I didn't think of it. I almost didn't want to watch the show, I was so excited about getting started. But I did anyway because when you love something as much as I love *Unlikely Heroes,* you just can't say no, especially if it is a new episode that you haven't seen before.

UNLIKELY HEROES SHOW

AND THEN I GRABBED HER ARM.

MEOW

MAN TALKING ABOUT HOW HE SAVED HIS MOM FROM FALLING OFF A BOAT WHEN SHE TRIPPED. IT WAS A CRUISE SHIP-TYPE BOAT.

TV SET

REALLY AMAZING BECAUSE HE IS IN A WHEELCHAIR.

THE DOG LIST

After the show, Max wanted to teach us how to do cartwheels, but we were too excited to work on our dog list to learn. Max loves to teach people to do new things, so he was disappointed that we were not in love with his cartwheel idea. I knew he was sad, so I said, "When we get a dog, you can teach it to do a flip." This made him happy and he said he was going to go home and look up dog tricks on his computer.

I didn't say anything about it, but I think it is a lot easier to teach a little dog to do a flip than a big dog. I don't even know if big dogs can do flips.

When he was gone, Mimi and I got started on a chart. We hadn't met any dogs yet so we just made a list of little and big dog things. The first things we wrote down were the good and the bad about each kind of dog.

BIG   LITTLE

BIG DOG GOOD	BIG DOG BAD	LITTLE DOG GOOD	LITTLE DOG BAD
① CAN USE DOG AS A PILLOW.	① LOTS OF FUR EVERYWHERE.	① CAN CARRY DOG IF HE GETS TIRED.	① TOO SMALL TO BE COZY WITH.
② CAN PROTECT YOU.	② BIG POOPS.	② SMALL POOPS.	② NOT AS MUCH DOG TO LOVE.
③ MORE DOG TO LOVE.	③ MAKES MORE MESS.	③ DOES NOT GET IN THE WAY.	③ LITTLE DOGS BARK MORE.
④ NICE-SOUNDING BARK.	④ HARDER TO GIVE A BATH TO.	④ CAN SIT IN YOUR LAP	④ YAPPY BARK.
⑤ CAN SWIM.	⑤ TAKES UP MORE OF YOUR BED.	⑤ NOT AS MUCH FUR.	⑤ LOTS OF LITTLE DOGS DON'T SWIM.

Mimi had some really good big-dog reasons, but still my mind was not changed. I don't think she liked my number-two reason about why little dogs were better. But it was something that was true, so she couldn't take it off the list. The only person who would maybe even be excited about the number-two reason at all was Sammy Stringer. He once did a whole photo project where he just took pictures of dog poop. When someone does something like that it is hard to forget it, even if you are starting to think he is maybe an okay person after all.

MY JOURNAL

I started on my journal writing, and it was surprisingly easy to write four sentences. One of my sentences was even super long because I had so much to put in it. I cannot believe that some of the kids in my class were complaining about having to do journal writing. I am going to work on my journal every night after dinner when there is nothing else going on. When there is daylight, too much stuff is happening, and that makes it a lot harder to concentrate.

Mimi is my best friend in the whole world, though right now we are not getting along 100 percent. We are trying to pick a dog and we both want something different. I want a little dog because they are cuter and I think that Mom and Dad would maybe say yes to a small dog because then they wouldn't notice it so much. Mimi wants a big dog because she thinks they are cozier and you can use their bodies as a pillow.

AUGUSTINE DUPRE

Augustine Dupre is my grown-up French friend.

She is a flight attendant, and she lives in the fancy apartment that Dad made in our basement. There are lots of great things about Augustine Dupre, but the best thing is that she is a great listener when you have a problem you want to talk about. If you don't have a problem, then she is still fun and interesting to talk to, because she is full of amazing stories about her trips to France. She goes to France almost every week.

Mom doesn't like me going downstairs to the basement at night to talk to her. She says, "Augustine is probably tired from all her traveling, and I'm

AUGUSTINE DUPRE IN HER FLIGHT ATTENDANT UNIFORM

sure she does not have the energy to talk to an eight-year-old." Sometimes Mom just says the silliest things, because anyone knows it hardly takes up any energy at all to just talk.

IT'S OKAY TO BE SNEAKY IF YOU DON'T GET CAUGHT

When Mom was busy in the kitchen I snuck downstairs and knocked on Augustine Dupre's door. I have a special knock so she knows it's me—that way she doesn't have to shoo Crinkles out the window if he is visiting her. Crinkles loves Augustine Dupre, maybe even more than he loves Mrs. Luther, who is his owner. They both buy him treats, and you can tell it just by looking at him, because he is getting kind of fat. Augustine Dupre is not allowed to have any pets in her apartment, so when Crinkles is visiting her we have to keep it a secret. Dad made this rule while he was wearing his non–animal person outside shell. Once we get a dog he'll change his mind about Crinkles for sure.

Of course Augustine Dupre is an animal person, and it turns out that she is not just a cat person, but a dog person too. She loved my idea about getting a dog to share with Mimi. It's a good thing that Crinkles does not really understand people talk, because he would not have been so happily sitting on

Augustine Dupre's lap if he knew we were trying to bring a dog into our lives. Some cats can kind of like dogs, but Crinkles does not look like that kind of cat.

CRINKLES MEETING A DOG

AUGUSTINE DUPRE'S IDEA

Augustine Dupre said that I had to show my parents that I was capable of taking care of a dog. *Capable* was her word, and since it seemed like it kind of meant the same sort of thing as *dependable*, it sounded like a good idea. *Capable* means you are able to do a certain thing, and the certain thing I had to do was to take care of a dog. This is not an easy thing to show someone you can do if you don't have a real dog to do it with. Augustine Dupre said there is a real difference between the saying you can do something and actually really doing the something.

HOW SHE GAVE ME HER IDEA

Sometimes when Augustine Dupre has an idea in her head she doesn't tell you in words what that idea is—instead, she likes to give you lots of hints. And then after enough hints, suddenly you know what she is talking about because her idea pops right into your head.

I could tell that she was doing this because I wanted to talk about dogs and she wanted to talk about other things. Usually she is happy to mostly talk about whatever I want to talk about. But this time she wanted to talk about the Crinkles postcard project that I made for Mrs. Luther and all the boxes I put together for the Lost poster project.

Then just before I was about to leave she said, "Yes, it's too bad you don't have some kind of dog so you could show your parents how you would care for it." I was feeling sad because this was true, but then just two seconds later Augustine Dupre's idea popped right into my head.

I was so excited, I shouted the idea out loud. "Wonderful!" said Augustine Dupre. "You are so clever." And then she gave me a big hug. Augustine Dupre always pretends the idea is 100 percent my idea, even if she did lots of helping to get me to think of it. I think she would be a very good teacher. Usually I don't like to leave her apartment, but this was not the way I was feeling with the new big idea in my head. I couldn't wait to get upstairs so I could tell Mimi about it.

Phone Rules

Mom has a rule about no starting phone calls after 8:00 p.m., so I couldn't call Mimi because it was already 8:10. If only I had figured out the big idea ten minutes earlier, everything would have been perfect. I'm actually allowed to talk on the phone until 8:15 if I started talking before 8:00. It seems like a silly rule, but it works okay. Mimi's mom liked it so much, she made it a rule at her house too. This is good, because it's kind of easier when friends have the same rules about stuff like the phone. I would feel bad if

Mimi was allowed to talk until 8:30 and we always had to stop at 8:15 just because of me.

MORSE CODE TALKING

As soon as I got to my room, I started wishing that I had been practicing the Morse code better. It was impossible to tell Mimi the whole dog idea with Morse code because it would take way too many words and that would be way too many flashes. I saw Mimi in her room, but it took forever before I could get her attention. Finally, she noticed me flashing my light at her window. The hard thing about the flashlight Morse code is that you have to do the dot parts really fast so that they don't get confused with the dash parts.

**THIS IS WHAT THE WORDS *DOG IDEA*
LOOK LIKE IN MORSE CODE.**

I had to do it twice because Mimi got confused the first time. I know this because we made up a signal for *confused*. You make big circles with your flashlight. This works out well, because it also sort of helps you feel better when you wave your arm around. I think it kind of gets the mad feelings out. It's too bad it's not the kind of thing you could do if you were mad and not in your room, because people would for sure think that you were crazy.

BREAKFAST

Mimi came over extra early at breakfast time because she wanted to know why I didn't want to get a dog anymore. She got the Morse code wrong and thought I had spelled out *nog idea* instead of *dog idea* like I really had. The *n* and the *d* are kind of close when you are using Morse code, and she had not seen one of my fast flashes.

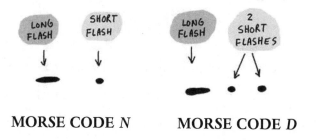

MORSE CODE *N*   **MORSE CODE *D***

Mimi said it took her a long time, but she finally decided that *nog* must be short for **not** "**o**" **g**ood, and so she thought I was saying *not* *"o" good idea* and was giving up on getting a dog. Mom heard us talking and said, "I sure wish she would give up on it." This was not a good thing. But Mimi was glad to hear that this was not true. On the way to school I told Mimi all about my new dog idea, and together we decided it was absolutely, marvelously brilliant!

SOMETIMES A DAY CAN LAST FOREVER

Mimi and I wanted school to be over so badly, because we couldn't wait to work on the new dog idea. School wanted to punish us for wanting to leave, so it made the day go extra super slow. I know that's not what really happened, but it sure felt like it. I had lunch with my two Graces and Mimi. Mimi and I were going to keep the whole picking-out-a-dog project a secret, but when you are totally 100 percent excited about something it is impossible to not talk about it. So we ended up telling the Graces about our big-dog little-dog list. Grace F. said she was only a little bit of a dog person, and Grace W. said she was a lot of a non–dog person.

GRACE F.

I ONLY LIKE SOME DOGS. I'M PICKY.

I DON'T REALLY LIKE DOGS AT ALL.

GRACE W.

One thing for sure is that you cannot tell if a person is a dog person or a non–dog person by just looking at her. Grace F. said she only liked some dogs, and it was lucky that Mr. Frank's dog, Winkie, was one of them, because it would be no fun to live next door to a dog that you didn't like. She invited both

Mimi and me to come over so we could meet Winkie and put him on our list. I think she felt a little bad that Winkie was a big dog and that she didn't have a wonderful little dog for me to put on the list too. That way both Mimi and I could be even. Mimi said she couldn't wait to meet Winkie and wouldn't it be great if he was the first dog at the top of our list. She was so excited and smiley about it that I had to say yes, even though I wanted to go straight home to work on my dog idea instead. Grace F. said it was okay to come over, so we decided to go to her house right after school. It was kind of on our way home, and I was hoping we'd maybe leave pretty quick—that way we would still have time to work on the dog idea before supper.

MIMI ALREADY BEING IN LOVE

Some Other Things That Happened at School

Miss Lois reminded us all not to forget to write in our journals. When she said that, Peter Marchelli put his hand up to his mouth and said, "Oops." Miss Lois didn't notice, but it was obvious that he had not even started on his journal project yet.

Max told Mimi that on the Internet it said that golden retriever–type dogs are very easy to train. This made Mimi even more excited about meeting Winkie.

Sammy Stringer asked me if it was true that I was getting a dog. When I said yes, he said, "But why?" This is not any easy question to answer, because there are all kinds of reasons why, and none of them was going to make any sense to Sammy because he was a non–dog person. So I didn't answer and instead just moved my shoulders up and down in the I-don't-know-why way. I remembered how Sammy had to wear oven mitts when he was going to touch Crinkles, and this made me imagine what his dog-touching outfit would look like.

SAMMY'S DOG-TOUCHNG OUTFIT

I guess I was smiling about it, because he said, "See if I care!" in a mad way and walked off. I think he thought I was making fun of him, which I was not. If you just think about something in your head it does not count as for real, and you are not allowed to get in trouble just for thinking things.

I noticed Grace L. staring at me and Mimi and the other Graces when we were eating lunch.

ONE DOG

If I was a lying type of person I'd say that Winkie is unfriendly, mean, stinky, ugly, and has really hard unsoft-type fur. But I'm not, so I had to write down the truth. He really is a wonderful dog, but he was big not only because he is a golden retriever–type dog, but because he is fat. I just know that Mom and Dad would never let me have a dog like that in our house, and especially not on my bed. He is not the kind of dog you could forget you had because he just kind of blended in with stuff. He is a stick-out dog, a supersizer! I tried to tell Mimi that we couldn't go from being a no-dog house to being a monster-size dog house all at once, but she wouldn't listen.

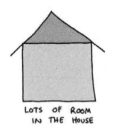

LOTS OF ROOM IN THE HOUSE

NO DOG IN THE HOUSE

NOT SO MUCH ROOM IN THE HOUSE BECAUSE THE DOG IS TAKING UP SO MUCH SPACE. IT IS HARD TO NOT NOTICE THIS DOG.

MONSTER-SIZE DOG IN THE HOUSE

TWO THINGS I DID NOT GET TO DO

At Grace F.'s house we did not see Mr. Frank, so I did not get to call him his not-in-school name of Jeffrey, and we did not get to see

Grace F.'s bedroom. The only part of the visit that worked out like I'd hoped was the leaving-pretty-quick part. Mimi and I got back to my house with lots of time to work on the dog idea before dinner. Mimi's sweatshirt was covered with Winkie's dog hair, but she didn't seem to mind it one little bit. I knew someone with the name of Mom who would not be excited about hair like that all over her house.

The first thing we did, before anything else, was put Winkie on our new dog chart. Max's idea was much better than just a big-dog-versus-little-dog list. After Mimi had written down all the good things about Winkie on the good side of the list, I added my two things to the bad side. Mimi let me draw the picture of Winkie, because drawing is one of the things I like to do more than she does.

NAME OF DOG	GOOD THINGS	BAD THINGS
Winkie Golden retriever type	Friendly, cozy, smart, soft fur, likes to play, gives ball back when playing catch, and can sit if you tell him to.	Loses lots of his fur all over your clothes. Would fill up too much of your house.

MY DOG IDEA

Mimi and I started on the idea as soon as we finished putting Winkie on the chart. It took a lot of cardboard and a lot of tape, but when we were finished we were really happy with how it turned out. The shape of it was just like a real dog. Then, after we painted it, it looked even better. We didn't plan it that way, but it turned out to be a medium-size dog, not big, not little, more just in the middle, and because of that both Mimi and I loved it the same.

OUR PRETEND DOG

BEFORE PAINTING   **AFTER PAINTING**

Sometimes the most fun part of a project is the making-stuff part, but this was not true this time. I could hardly wait to show him to Mom and Dad, and then after that to start using him as if he were a real dog. Both Mimi and I decided he was a boy dog and not a girl dog. I don't know why, but he just was. We were going to name him Box Dog, but then Mimi said we should try to think of something cute so my mom and dad would like him better. That was a really good idea for her to think of, and one that was going to help us for sure.

DOG NAMES WE THOUGHT OF

Pepper

Sparky

Spotty

Coffee

(Mimi thought we could name it this because my mom loves coffee so much, but then I reminded her that my dad hates coffee, so we had to do more thinking.)

Pie

We named the box dog Pie (because everybody in my family loves pie), but then after about three minutes I thought of something else even better. I got the idea because Mimi said the name should be something cute, and we wanted it to be something that both Mom and Dad really loved. Sometimes you think you have a great idea and then— surprise!—an even better idea comes along.

When I was little I loved ketchup. I still like it, but I guess back then I had trouble saying the name right. Mom and Dad love to tell the story of how instead of saying "ketchup," I called it "chip-up." Mom says it was one of the cutest things she ever heard. Even now, every time we have ketchup, Mom and Dad talk about the chip-up story. After I told this all to Mimi, she said we definitely had to name our dog Chip-Up. Just doing that was going to help us a ton.

INTRODUCING CHIP-UP

I asked Mom if Mimi could stay for dinner, and of course she said yes. I was a little bit nervous about showing Chip-Up to Mom and Dad, so it was nice to have Mimi there to help. Right before dinner we put a bowl down on the kitchen floor next to Chip-Up so he could have dinner too. It didn't take long for Mom to notice him, and when we told her his name she even made the cute *awww* sound. Dad liked him too. He said Chip-Up looked very well proportioned, which means he thought we did a good job

KETCHUP ON TABLE

CHIP-UP ON FLOOR

making his legs and body and head all the right sizes.

After dinner we took Chip-Up outside to go to the bathroom, because that is the kind of thing a real dog owner would have to do. We were going to take him for a walk, but he didn't slide very well on the sidewalk. I was worried that he would get all ripped up, so I picked him up and carried him. Good thing he wasn't a real dog or he would have been really heavy and probably squirmy too. Chip-Up of course was perfectly behaved! It was also kind of nice not to have to pick up real dog poop.

**ME CARRYING
CHIP-UP**

JOURNAL TIME AGAIN

After Mimi left I took Chip-Up to my room, but it took a while for me to decide where to put him. Finally I put him on the bed next to me, because that is where a real dog would probably want to go. I put him on his side so he could be more comfy and maybe even sleepy, but he didn't look like either of those things because his legs were sticking out sideways. It looked much more real and better after I covered him up with the quilt that Grandma made me. He was kind of cute, and looked all cozy with just his little head sticking out. It was hard to stop touching and playing with him and concentrate on my journal writing. I wonder if that happens with real dogs too? I wonder if the kids in my class who have real dogs have trouble con-

centrating and doing their homework? I wonder if they would rather play with their dog
instead of write in their journal like they are
supposed to?

*Today I have a new dog in my life. His
name is Chip-Up, and he is the most well-
behaved dog in the world. He is going to
help Mimi and me get a real dog in our
lives. I can tell that my mom and dad are
already falling in love with him.*

I really, really wanted to take Chip-Up
downstairs and introduce him to Augustine
Dupre, but there was no way that Mom was
not going to notice me when I had a box dog

following me down the stairs, so we just stayed in my room. I wonder if real dogs make it hard for you to be sneaky too?

WHAT WE DID BEFORE BED

Chip-Up watched me take a bath, he helped me clean up my room, and then right before bed we both waved good night to Mimi, who was perfectly looking out her window at exactly the right time. I was tired, so I'm glad Mimi wasn't wanting to start any flashlight talking. Flashlight talking is not like regular talking. It takes a lot more of your energy.

ME AND CHIP-UP IN MY BED

WHERE CHIP-UP WAS IN THE MORNING

I bet a real dog would be a lot more cozy to sleep with than Chip-Up was. His edges were pointy, and he was taking up a lot of the bed with his very pokey body. In the middle of the night I had to push him onto the floor. I was glad he wasn't a real dog because I would have felt pretty bad about that if he was. But still I felt a little guilty, so I said, "I'm sorry, Chip-Up," even though he couldn't understand me or care.

SAMMY'S GREAT IDEA

I took Chip-Up outside to go to the bathroom before I even had any of my breakfast. It seemed sort of silly since he really wasn't going to do anything, but like Augustine

Dupre said, it was the showing part that was important. While I was outside standing around, Sammy came by with our newspaper. He used to deliver the paper late, but Max said people were starting to complain, so he is trying harder to be on time. He seemed really happy to see me and Chip-Up, and he stopped his bike right in our driveway.

"Oh, I thought you were getting a real dog," said Sammy. "Did you make him?"

I didn't want to make Sammy nervous, so I didn't say anything about Chip-Up one day turning into a real dog. "Mimi and I did it. His name is, uh . . . Chip-Up." I was surprised, but Sammy was acting like he was really impressed! And then he surprised me even more with a great idea when I wasn't even looking for one.

"You can borrow my skateboard if you want. If you tape his feet to it, you can pull

him around with you
and stuff."

 SAMMY'S SKATEBOARD

Most people in the world would think it was totally weird for a girl to be standing outside on her front grass in her pajamas with a dog made out of boxes, but not Sammy. He liked weird things. Weird things were normal to him. And then for the first time ever in my whole entire life I thought, *Am I weird too?* This is not the best thing to suddenly start thinking about first thing in

 the morning, but Sammy didn't notice. "I'll bring the board over to Max's later," said Sammy, and then he rode away.

After our breakfast, mine real and Chip-Up's pretend, we went downstairs to see Augustine Dupre. She answered her door in a fancy red robe that matched her red curtains

perfectly, which was no surprise because she always looks excellent. Of course she noticed Chip-Up right away—she is good like that. "I love it! It's perfect!" she said, and then she gave me a hug. As much as Augustine Dupre loved Chip-Up, Crinkles hated Chip-Up. He backed up into the fridge and started growling and hissing and poofed his fur up so he looked even fatter than he really was. I was right about him: Crinkles is 100 percent not a dog-liking cat! I would have stayed longer, but Augustine Dupre said I should probably leave before Crinkles had a heart attack. It was kind of nice to think that Chip-Up looked so good that Crinkles thought he was

real. I was definitely going to tell Mimi about that part.

WHAT HAPPENED AT SCHOOL THAT WAS EXCITING

Nothing.

SCHOOL VERSUS AFTER SCHOOL

1 School is more exciting than after school.
2 School is the same amount of exciting as after school.
3 School and after school are both not exciting.
4 School is less exciting than after school.

When Mr. Frank was our teacher, we had a lot of number 1 and number 2 days. Now with just Miss Lois, we are getting a lot more number 4 days. It would be great if she could put some more of the number 2 days back.

BEFORE THE DOG PARK

Mimi and I couldn't wait to get out of school so we could go to the park and meet some more dogs for our list. Of course Mimi wanted a full report on Chip-Up and everything that had happened after she went home the night before. I think she was a little sad that she couldn't have Chip-Up at her house too, but that was not part of the project. Chip-Up had to stay with me so that Mom and Dad could see my responsibility parts working. When I told her about Sammy Stringer's skateboard idea, she loved it. She wanted to put Chip-Up on the skateboard right away so we could take him to the park with us to meet the other dogs. After school we went to Max's house to get the skateboard, but Sammy hadn't dropped it off yet. Max wanted to see Chip-Up so much that we had to take him to my house to meet him even though we were in a big rush to get to the park. This was a lucky thing because I was totally forgetting about having to take Chip-Up outside to go to the bathroom before we left.

While we were outside, Max tried to throw Chip-Up around like he was doing flips and tricks. I was glad when Mimi got mad and said, "You have to treat Chip-Up like he's a real dog! Would you throw a real dog into the air? I sure hope not!" It's not fun to be with Mimi when she is angry. I guess Max knows that too, because right away he said he was sorry and that he didn't know there were rules about Chip-Up. This was a good thing to do, because Mimi was instantly smiling again and she even invited him to come to the park with us. Chip-Up couldn't come because he didn't have his wheels yet and none of us wanted to carry him all that way. If he was a real dog I am sure he would have been bark-

ing and yelping with unhappiness because he was tied to the front porch and was being left behind. Sometimes it was a good thing that he was only made of cardboard.

THE DOG PARK

There were so many dogs at the dog park, we could hardly decide who we should go and meet first, and then by the end we didn't even meet all of them. The owner people thought it was interesting that we were writing down notes, and were extra friendly and helpful about telling us lots of information about their dogs.

My favorite dog of the whole park was a little Jack Russell–type dog named Emma. Even Mimi liked her. She was super cute and super smart. One of her favorite things to do was to chase a soccer ball. If you kicked it she would chase it and bring it right back to you by pushing it with her nose. Max said that that kind of dog can for sure do a flip, because he had seen one do it in a commercial on TV.

When we got home Mimi and I went inside to add all the new dogs to the chart. Max went home to see if the skateboard was there.

DOG CHART PART 2

NAME OF DOG	GOOD THINGS	BAD THINGS
Winkie Golden retriever type	Friendly, cozy, smart, soft fur, likes to play, gives ball back when playing catch, and can sit if you tell him to.	Loses lots of his fur all over your clothes. Would fill up too much of your house.
Emma Jack Russell type	Smart, funny, friendly, cute, and soft	Can't think of one bad thing!
Flash Bulldog type	Mostly liked chewing on sticks. Loved to chase sticks too.	Did not really like the other dogs. Was droolly and looked really heavy.

NAME OF DOG	GOOD THINGS	BAD THINGS
Morgan Cocker spaniel type	Liked the other dogs a lot. Had extra- soft, cozy ears. Chased the ball and mostly brought it back.	Its fur was kind of dirty and its owner said it needed lots of baths and brushing.
Penny Mixed dog	Would chase squirrels out of your yard.	Didn't care about being petted.
Bernie Mixed dog	Was very friendly and liked to play ball and chase the other dogs.	Fur was not super soft.
Oakley Labrador type	Wanted to chase the ball forever.	Did not want to be petted for very long. Did not like other dogs.

NAME OF DOG	GOOD THINGS	BAD THINGS
Cougar Labrador mixed	Loved to be petted and loved watching the other dogs.	Seemed like he was really sleepy because he did a lot of lying down.
Mika German shepherd mix	Was super smart, could even do tricks. Liked people more than dogs.	Can't think of one bad thing except that she was a big dog.

Writing a chart about dogs is a lot of work and a very tiring project, especially if you are the one who still has to draw all the pictures of the dogs at the end of the doing the words part. Mimi was nice and went downstairs to get us a snack from my kitchen while I was doing all the drawing.

She took Chip-Up with her because she said she wanted to do some practicing of taking care of a dog in a house.

When she got back it was almost time for supper, so it was a good thing that Mom did not see her taking the cookies off the counter. Moms don't like it if you eat four or five cookies when there are only about ten minutes until suppertime, even if you are totally and completely 100 percent starving so you would eat all the food on your plate at supper anyway.

I could tell that Mimi was loving Chip-Up because she asked me to put him on my window ledge at night. That way she could see him if she looked at my window from her house. She put him there to show me how perfectly he would fit, but he fell off onto the floor and squished one of his ears. Mimi felt really bad about that and was about to cry until I reminded her to remember that he was only a cardboard dog, so he couldn't really be hurt.

She still told him she was sorry and we tried to fix his ear. Mimi put him on my bed and I put a cover over him so we couldn't see his legs sticking out funny on the side. "He looks comfy," said Mimi, and that made her feel a whole ton better.

WHAT HAPPENED AT DINNER

I was halfway finished with my supper when I remembered that Chip-Up was upstairs resting and I had forgotten to bring him down so he could eat too. It was really important to do the suppertime thing because that was one of the ways that Mom and Dad were going to see for themselves my responsibility.

"Oh, I see that Chip-Up is back," said Mom. Then Dad said, "A responsible dog owner wouldn't forget to feed her dog dinner." This was not something I wanted him to say, and I especially didn't want him to start using his favorite *irresponsible* word on me. So I said, "A real dog would be easier because he would follow me everywhere I went, and at suppertime he'd stand right next to me drooling, so I could never forget to feed him, even if I wanted to, which I wouldn't! Chip-Up is harder to take care of because I have to do all the owner stuff, plus then I have to remember to do all the dog parts too."

Mom was smiling and nodding her head up and down, which meant that she was thinking that I was 100 percent right. But then Dad said, "Well, that may be true, but you have to remember that there are many things that your Chip-Up doesn't do that a real dog would. Things like bark when you want him to be quiet, chew on things he shouldn't, demand to be taken out for walk . . . right?"

When a dad gives you a whole list of things you didn't think of before, it can be hard to think of the right thing to say back. Sometimes it can be so hard to think that your stomach, which was so very hungry before the list, now says, "No more food, please." This is what happened to me.

BACK TO MY JOURNAL, SORT OF

Dad has ruined all my filled-with-excitement feelings and good thoughts about the Chip-Up project. This is what I wanted to write in my journal, but then I remembered the part about Miss Lois reading it and I didn't want her to think Dad was mean and bad, even if I was thinking those things. I was feeling so yucky, I didn't even want to write about dogs at all, even though Emma was looking like one of the best dogs on the whole list and she was a small dog, so I should have been super happy. The other good dog was Mika, and of course that one was Mimi's favorite because she was big. It was hard to say anything bad about Mika because it wasn't her fault she had grown up to be big. If she were small I would have for sure loved her as much as I loved Emma. But I didn't feel like writing about any of this in my journal. Instead I wrote about the only thing that I didn't really have to think about, and it was for sure not going to be interesting when I was old and forgetting about my life now, but I didn't care.

Today I had toast with butter and jam for breakfast. I also had a half glass of orange juice, which is not my favorite, but Mom says I have to drink it because it is healthy. I just saw Mrs. Witkins climbing into her very own house through her basement window. This is weird because I can see her whole family watching something on TV upstairs, so it's not because she is locked out of her house.

MRS. WITKINS'S HOUSE

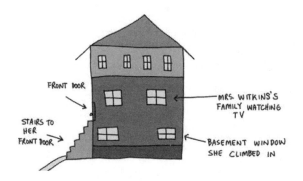

FRONT DOOR

STAIRS TO
HER
FRONT DOOR →

MRS. WITKINS'S
FAMILY WATCHING
TV

BASEMENT WINDOW
SHE CLIMBED IN

It was a good thing that I looked out my window when I heard Oliver bark, or I would have missed her. Mrs. Witkins lives next door to Mr. Hurley and Oliver across the street. Anytime someone steps even close to Mr. Hurley's house, Oliver starts barking. He is not very friendly, but he is a very good watchdog. Oliver must have heard Mrs. Witkins trying to climb in the window. Mrs. Witkins is a very nice lady, but she is not someone who you would think would be climbing through windows in the night. She is not very sporty. She is definitely not a rock-climbing-type mom or even a jumping-around-type mom. She is a sewing-and-cooking-type mom, so this was for sure something very strange that was going on.

OLIVER'S DREAM PRESENT

I watched for a long time, but nothing more happened except that Mr. Hurley took Oliver for a walk. Oliver loves to eat all kinds of garbage from the street, so Mr. Hurley is always trying to pull disgusting things out of Oliver's mouth before he can swallow them.

Mimi and I would have to be careful not to pick a dog like that. I watched for Mrs. Witkins some more, but I couldn't even see her in the basement, so it was kind of boring. Maybe she went out a different window that I couldn't see.

MR. HURLEY'S HOUSE

MRS. WITKINS'S HOUSE

Tomorrow I was definitely going to tell Mimi about Mrs. Witkins so we could both watch from our windows to see if she did it again. Then I drew a funny little comic for Mimi so we could remember about not picking a dog that eats garbage.

COMIC FOR MIMI

THE OTHER GRACE

Grace L. was looking at me again in class. I think either she really wants to be friends with us other Graces or she doesn't like me.

It's hard to tell, because she is not a very smi-ley-type person.

WHAT HAPPENED AT SCHOOL TODAY

Sammy Stringer said he is 100 percent going to bring his skateboard over after school today. That is good because then at least we can tape Chip-Up to it and take him for a walk. That'll be one of the new three things that Dad said a real dog would do. We'll have to make sure that Mom sees us so she can tell Dad all about it.

Mimi said that tonight we definitely have to watch and see if Mrs. Witkins climbs in

 her basement window again. It happened around eight o'clock last night, so that is when we are going to do our spying.

Miss Lois reminded us that we must not give up on our journal writing. Then she told us about some famous people who kept journals and how those journals were important today because they told us things about history and life from a long time ago that we might not normally know about. Now we have cameras and video, so journal writing is probably not so needed anymore, but I didn't say that out loud because I could tell that Miss Lois would not be happy to hear it.

FAMOUS PEOPLE WHO HAVE DONE JOURNAL WRITING

Lewis and Clark were two really important explorers who traveled from Pittsburgh, Pennsylvania, by land all the way to the Pacific Ocean and back again. They were the first explorers to do this and it took them a really long time, almost three years. Back in 1803 when they did this there were no cars or railroads, and of course no planes, so they had to walk the whole way. They kept a journal of all the things they saw and all the adventures they had. This was important because when we read it today we can know what life was like way back then, since everybody from then is now dead and can't tell us about it.

Beatrix Potter, who was a famous writer and drawer of children's books, started a journal when she was fifteen years old and wrote in it every day until she was about thirty years old. The cool thing about her was that she wrote her whole journal in a secret code so that even if other people found it they would never be able to read it. I am sure she didn't use flashlight Morse code because that would have taken her forever and then she wouldn't have had time to write all her books. She wrote lots of stories with bunnies and little animals that had adventures and could talk, such as Peter Rabbit.

The last person that Miss Lois told us about was Samuel Pepys. She said he had one of the most famous journals ever. He lived in London, England, in the 1660s and kept a journal about everything that happened in his life. This was a big deal, because he wrote about the Great London Fire of 1666 and about the Great Plague of London in 1665.

Plague is a bad sickness that kills most people who get it. His journal must have been very sad because he was writing about a lot of dying. If I had to write about people dying I would for sure be crying. I wonder if his journal has tears on the pages. I was going to ask Miss Lois but was interrupted by Valerie Newcome, who started talking right away in front of me and didn't even put her hand up.

**ME GIVING VALERIE A MEAN LOOK BUT
I DON'T THINK SHE NOTICED**

Valerie Newcome said that journal writing was exciting to her because she was planning on being famous when she grew up, so her journals would probably be worth lots of money and be really interesting for everyone to read. Martin, the boy who sits behind her, said, "Famous for what?" But before Valerie could answer, Miss Lois said we all had to calm down, and she started talking about Samuel Pepys again, which was not as exciting as Miss Lois thought it was.

I stopped paying attention and started doodling, and I don't know why but it turned into a little cartoon about Valerie being famous. It wasn't a very nice comic, but I didn't really do it on purpose. It just came out that way.

Miss Lois saw that I wasn't paying attention, and before I could hide my paper she took it from me. The next words she said were the most horrible words you would never want to hear.

THE MOST HORRIBLE WORDS

Miss Lois said, "Just Grace, you will take this and report to the principal's office!" Mr. Harris is nice, but he's the principal so he is still scary, and it is especially no fun to sit on the black chair outside his office. Everyone who sees you there gives you the you-are-in-so-much-trouble look. Mrs. M. is extra good at the look, and this is especially bad because she is the office helper who sits right across from the black chair, so she can give you the look a lot!

WHAT MR. HARRIS SAID

Mr. Harris looked at my comic and said, "So, can you tell me about this?" I was glad to be able to do some explaining, because I wanted him to know that it was an accident and that I didn't really mean to be mean on purpose, and that maybe Valerie would be famous one day and then everyone would need to know that she used to make Barbie clothes out of see-through tape and somehow that would be important for history. I was happy when he said that he understood that part.

But then he said that the part he did not understand was why I was drawing a comic when I should have been paying attention in class. This was the part that I was not ready to do any explaining about, because you can't tell a principal that you think your teacher is boring.

So I said, "I'm sorry. I won't do it again." "Good, glad to hear it," said Mr. Harris. And then he said that he was going to throw away my comic so that no one else could see it, but that he wanted me to draw him a new one for the next day about something I had learned in class. Something about journals, and something that was not mean-spirited, which is a word that means making fun of people so they get their feelings hurt. Then he sent me back to Miss Lois.

SLOW, SAD WALK BACK TO MY CLASS

SOMETHING THAT IS HARD BUT NOT IMPOSSIBLE

It is hard to walk back into your classroom after you have gotten in trouble at the principal's office. It would be better if it was impossible—then you wouldn't have to do it—but it's not. Miss Lois said I could take my seat, and everyone stared at me as I did it! I kept my eyes looking at my desk for the whole rest of the time until lunch because I didn't want to see anyone looking at me.

As soon as the bell rang for lunch Mimi rushed over to my desk to ask about what had happened. I could have told her the whole long truth but I didn't. Instead I said, "I'm not allowed to doodle anymore while I'm in class." That way she didn't even ask about the comic, which I wished I had never drawn in the first place. Sometimes if you try hard enough you can almost pretend something never happened, especially if there are only three people in the whole world who know about it.

ME

MISS LOIS

MR. HARRIS

CHIP-UP'S FIRST WALK

It was nice that everyone was so super excited about Chip-Up. It made it easier to forget about my bad day. Max and Sammy watched while Mimi and I did the taping of his legs to the skateboard. And before we all left for the park I made sure to yell to Mom that I was taking Chip-Up for a walk. Chip-Up was easy to pull because Sammy had a really nice skateboard with good wheels. Sammy said he wasn't sure if he was going to stay with us at the park, and I knew that was because he  was not happy about meeting any real dogs. I couldn't wait to introduce Chip-Up to Emma.

THE PARK

When we got to the park, none of the real dogs wanted to meet Chip-Up. They were all too busy chasing balls and playing with other real dogs. Emma wasn't there so I couldn't tell if she was going to be interested in Chip-Up or not. Sammy said he'd stay with Chip-Up if we wanted to go and visit with the real dogs, and I knew that was because he did not want to be near large furry animals. Mimi and I met three new dogs to add to our list but they were not as wonderful as Emma, or as smart as Mika, or as sweet as Winkie, though they were skinnier. The dog owners who we had met before were all happy to see us and were all talking together like they were the people part of the dog club. Two girls who were young like us were there too.

Their dog was just a puppy so they couldn't let him go off the leash because he wasn't trained yet and would probably run away. Dog people seem to be very friendly, maybe even friendlier than cat people, but that's kind of hard to tell for sure because cats don't really like to hang out with other cats, so their people can't hang out together either.

WHAT DAD ASKED FOR

On the way home I told Mimi, Max, and Sammy what Dad had said about Chip-Up not really being a very good example for taking care of a dog because he didn't do that many real dog things. "You need to make him more real," said Max. "Have him do more real dog stuff." "Maybe you should pretend harder," said Mimi. "You know, make it a bigger deal." Sammy didn't say anything, probably because he didn't want me to get a real dog anyway.

When we got to my house we took Chip-Up off the skateboard and I took him inside because it was suppertime, and supper-pretend-time with Chip-Up.

THE SHOW

All through dinner I did lots of talking to Chip-Up. I told him not to beg, I told him to sit (even though his legs didn't bend right so he couldn't do it anyway), and I told him to lie down and stop whining. I even made some whiny noises so it would sound more real. Mom was having a hard time not laughing, and that was okay because it was kind of funny, and all I wanted anyway was for Dad to be paying attention.

After dinner Chip-Up and I rolled around in the living room making lots of noise. Then Chip-Up jumped up on the couch and got in trouble and had to sit in the corner. This pretending was turning out to be a lot more fun than I thought it would be. I don't know why, but Chip-Up was in a very naughty mood.

When I wasn't looking—so
it really wasn't my fault
because I couldn't stop him—he went and
chewed up Dad's shoelaces.

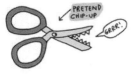

He got sent to the backyard for that,
because as a good dog owner, which I am, I
know behavior like that is just not acceptable!

After a while I forgave him, and I'm pretty sure he knows never to do that kind of
thing again. I was having so much fun with
Chip-Up that I almost completely missed
looking out my window at eight o'clock. It
was good luck that I heard Oliver barking,
because that reminded me about it.

MRS. WITKINS

Mrs. Witkins was standing at the bottom of
her stairs, waving to her daughter Emily, who
is older than I am so we don't know each

other. After Emily closed the door, Mrs. Witkins started walking down the street, and I thought for sure she was not going to do the window-sneaking thing again. But as soon as she passed Mr. Hurley's house she turned back around and walked through his yard to get to her window. Of course Oliver was going crazy with barking. I was hoping that Mimi was looking because Mrs. Witkins is not a very good window climber and that made it 100 percent funnier to watch. Just like the time before, the last thing I saw was Mrs. Witkins's bottom disappearing through the window.

As soon as that happened I went to my side window to see if Mimi was there. Of course she was, and she was waving her flashlight around to try to get me to notice her. I turned my flashlight on and held Chip-Up next to me so she could see him.

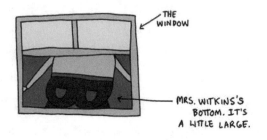

THE WINDOW

MRS. WITKINS'S BOTTOM. IT'S A LITTLE LARGE.

Right away Mimi started flashing her light to tell me she wanted to send me a message. I had to put Chip-Up down so I could write out the Morse code she was sending me.

It always takes me longer than it takes Mimi to figure out what a message says. I think my brain gets confused with all the dots and dashes. This time it took twenty-five minutes to figure out her message, but most of that time was taken up with looking for my Morse code chart, which probably got knocked off when Chip-Up fell off my window, because where I found it was under my bed.

WHAT MIMI'S MESSAGE SAID

Funny

Mostly I think flashlight Morse code might be just too hard to ever be fun.

WHY I CAN'T GO TO BED

Miss Lois was right: It's much easier to work on your journal if you do it the same time every night. I had a little thought that maybe I should write something nice about Valerie—that way when Miss Lois read it she would know that the comic I made was a mistake and that I wasn't trying on purpose to make fun of Valerie and that it was really just something that was unfortunate. But then that reminded me of the comic I still had to make for Mr. Harris. And since I couldn't think of anything special to say about Valerie that didn't sound dumb and not true anyway, I decided to write about Mrs. Witkins again instead. I was going to describe her house and where the basement window was, so I looked out and guess who I saw climbing back out of the very same basement window?

Mrs. Witkins is my across-the-street neighbor. Every night at around eight o'clock she leaves her house and pretends to walk down the street, and then she sneaks back and climbs into her very own basement window. At about 8:45 she climbs back out the window and goes up the stairs and into the house through her front door. She seems to be very sneaky!

I was hoping that Miss Lois was not going to think I was being mean by saying that Mrs. Witkins was sneaky. I on purpose left out the part about her being kind of tubby and having trouble fitting in the window, because it sounded like I was maybe making fun of her, and I for certain did not want to get in trouble again. Just thinking about being sent to Mr. Harris's office was making me all sad in my stomach again.

HOW TO USE A FLASHLIGHT AT NIGHT

Dad came into my room to say good night and said I had to go directly to bed because it was way past my bedtime and tomorrow was a school day. I couldn't tell him about Mr. Harris's comic because it is not a normal thing to have to draw a comic for the school's principal and he would have for sure been full of questions about wondering why.

If I did not have to, I was not going to tell him about getting into trouble at school. Girls who get in trouble at school do not get to have a present of a real dog in their life. I know that 100 percent.

After he left I put on my pajamas, made Chip-Up a bed on the floor, and said good night to Mom. I had to turn off my light because both Mom and Dad have light-bulb sensors in their brains. They would notice the light being on and catch me not sleeping in seconds. They are like superheroes about light.

MY JOURNAL COMIC

I made a tent with the covers over my head and started to draw Mr. Harris's comic, using my flashlight so I could see.

NOT A GOOD WAY TO WAKE UP

I got woken up this morning because I heard Dad yelling something about shoes. I was lying in bed thinking *shoes* sounds a lot like *snooze,* which was something I wanted to do more of because I was so tired from staying up forever drawing Mr. Harris's comic.

Then suddenly I remembered Chip-Up and his chewing. In half a second I was 100 percent totally awake. Now I could hear Dad really well. "Why are my shoelaces chewed up? Will you look at this? I can't tie anything with this half-chewed lace! Do we have squirrels in this house? What's going on? Now I'm going to miss my train!"

I could hear Mom too—she was trying to keep Dad calm. "I don't know, dear. Here are your loafers. Wear these. I'm sure we'll figure it all out later. Have a good meeting, dear. See you later." And then nothing.

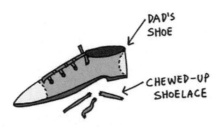

DAD'S SHOE

CHEWED-UP SHOELACE

THIS IS GOING TO BE A BAD DAY

Chip-Up and I went down the stairs really super quietly. I had to carry him because he makes a thump on each step if you pull him with his leash, and you can't sneak around with a thumping dog behind you. We went outside and stood on the front lawn for a little while, and I sort of wished it could be forever because I did not want to go into the kitchen and see Mom. Finally I had to be brave and go back inside. Mom didn't say anything, and for half a second I was hoping  that she thought that maybe there was a squirrel in the house too. But that was before she looked at Chip-Up and me and shook her head in a way that said, *Boy, I feel sorry for you, because you are going to be in so much trouble!*

CAN I STAY AT SCHOOL FOREVER?

Mimi and I walked to school together. She didn't have any great ideas about how to save my life.

I gave my comic to Mrs. M. because Mr. Harris wasn't in his office. She gave me her you-are-in-trouble look. It was as if she could tell that all the unluckiness in my life was in no way nearly over.

It's really hard to concentrate when you are waiting for bad things that you know are for sure going to happen. Miss Lois could tell that I wasn't paying good attention because she kept saying, "Just Grace, are you with us?" I was trying to think of something super special and great to do so that Dad would have to 100 percent lose his angry feelings.

It's not easy to think of super amazing get-out-of-trouble ideas. I couldn't think of anything.

On my way out of the school I noticed that Mr. Harris had taped my comic on his door. This was a total surprise and it made me smile for half a second. It was one lucky thing in a very unlucky-looking day.

NO SADNESS FOR ME

All the way home Mimi and Max and Sammy wanted to talk about taking Chip-Up to the park. They were not filled with sadness like I was, and they did not have any sympathy for me. Sympathy is when you feel bad because someone else feels bad and you want to show you care about that. All they cared about were dogs.

I was surprised that Sammy even wanted to go back to the park. When we got to my house I tried to stay outside on the front lawn for as long as I could. Max finally said, "Come on! Go get Chip-Up so we can go." Mimi offered to go with me because it's a fact that a parent yells at you less if you have a friend standing right next to you. As soon as we walked into the kitchen, because Max and Sammy wanted us to bring a snack too, Mom said, "Your father is working late tonight." That was two lucky things. Now all I wanted was one more lucky thing, and that last lucky thing was a not-mad Dad.

THE WALK TO THE DOG PARK

We taped Chip-Up to the skateboard, gave out the crackers, and then finally we were walking to the park. When we walked past Mrs. Witkins's house, I totally remembered that I had forgotten to tell Mimi about Mrs. Witkins coming back out the window. So I told the whole story to Max and Sammy too so they would know what we were talking about. It's good manners to include every-one in a conversation if you can remember to do it.

Sammy said it would be cool if Mrs. Witkins was a spy. I said I didn't think she looked like she could do any cool spy stuff because even getting in the window seemed like it was hard for her to do. Plus, who would she be spying on, anyway? Her family? Sammy said, "Yeah, I guess you're right, but still, it would be cool if it was true."

He was right about that, but it was too hard to imagine that it could be true. Mrs. Witkins was definitely not like an M&M. She was not a superspy underneath and a regular mom on top. You could just tell about that.

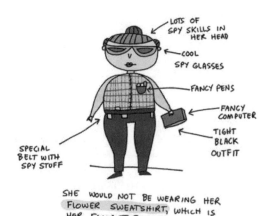

LOTS OF
SPY SKILLS IN
HER HEAD

COOL
SPY GLASSES

FANCY PENS

FANCY
COMPUTER

TIGHT
BLACK
OUTFIT

SPECIAL
BELT WITH
SPY STOFF

SHE WOULD NOT BE WEARING HER
FLOWER SWEATSHIRT, WHICH IS
HER FAVORITE BECAUSE SHE WEARS
IT A LOT.

IF MRS. WITKINS WAS A SPY

DOG THOUGHTS

"I hope Emma will be there!" I said. I wanted to talk about something that was 100 percent for sure good. "Me too," said Max. "Her owner said he's going to help me teach her how to do a flip." Mimi and Sammy didn't say anything, probably because Mimi was thinking big-dog thoughts, and Sammy was thinking no-dog thoughts, and both those thoughts were not really group thoughts right now at that moment.

THE WORST DOG EVER

Sometimes a day can start off bad, but then other things happen and you think that maybe in the end you will be lucky and it will not be so bad after all. This is the kind of day I was hoping I would get, but this was not what happened, because as soon as Emma saw Chip-Up rolling in the park, she attacked him!

First she tried to bite the skateboard wheels as I was trying to pull him away, and then she grabbed Chip-Up's leg. She had it in her teeth and she was shaking it so hard, she pulled him right off the skateboard. She would have run away with his whole entire body except that Sammy was brave and grabbed Chip-Up's middle. Emma was growling and we were all screaming—it was terrible! Emma had Chip-Up's leg in her mouth and no matter how hard Sammy pulled on Chip-Up she wouldn't let go. Finally she ripped his whole complete leg right off his body! Emma turned around and took off with it. Max tried to catch her, but she was too sneaky and speedy for him. She ran to the middle of the park and chewed it up until there was nothing left but little pieces of litter. I couldn't believe it! She was Horrible!

CHIP-UP'S LEG

WHO IS VERY SORRY NOW

Mr. Scott, who is the man that owns Emma, said he was sorry about a billion times and we could tell he felt really guilty that his dog had turned into a crazy, horrible creature. It took him forever to get Emma back on her leash. I guess her two favorite games are soccer and chase me. Max helped chase her down while Mimi and I inspected Chip-Up. We were too surprised about what had happened to even cry. Sammy went to pick up the little pieces of Chip-Up's leg because he is good about not littering, and all the dog park

COMPLETELY
SQUISHED EARS

LEG
MISSING

BENT UP

people were coming over to us with their dogs and Sammy didn't want to be close to any dogs. Chip-Up looked terrible. His new name could be Rip-Up!

Mr. Scott offered to pay to get Chip-Up fixed, but since Mimi and I just made him out of cardboard we couldn't take any money. Everyone was super nice and trying to make us feel better with their words. Finally someone asked why we had made Chip-Up in the first place.

It was nice to talk about something different because all the sorry talking was starting to make me feel like I was going to cry. I told them about how Chip-Up was going to show my parents I was responsible and dependable, and once that had happened they were going to have to buy me a real dog.

I think this made Mr. Scott feel even

worse because he started saying "I'm so sorry" again. The man that owns Bernie said he had some ideas to help and that he wanted us to come back to the park tomorrow to talk about them. Mimi was holding Chip-Up and she was starting to cry, so we had to leave. It was a very sad walk home. By the time we got to my front door, I was crying too.

HOW CHIP-UP SAVED MY LIFE

Dad opened the door like he had maybe been waiting for me, and I guessed that he was, because he had his chewed-up shoelaces in his hand. What he saw was not at all what he had been expecting, because he dropped the shoelaces and said, "Grace, are you all right? Tell me what happened. What's wrong?"

And then I couldn't help it. I started crying so hard I couldn't even talk. Mom and Dad were really upset about Chip-Up. I was 100 percent surprised that they cared so much. They wanted to go back to the park and talk to Mr. Scott about Emma and her attacking ways. This was not something I wanted. Even though I was newly filled up with mean feelings about Emma, I didn't want her to get in trouble or have something bad happen to her.

It took a long time, but finally Mom and Dad said they would not complain to Mr. Scott. After supper Dad totally surprised me when he said he wanted to help me fix Chip-Up's leg. It was nice of him because he is much better at glueing and taping than I am. When Chip-Up had his parts all together again we put him on my bed. Then Dad said, "Now, Chip-Up, there will be no more shoelace chewing, or chewing of anything else in this house! Understood?" Of course Chip-Up couldn't say anything, so Dad looked at me. I was kind of too nervous to talk, so I just nodded my head up and down in the *yes* way. "Good," said Dad, and then he patted Chip-Up on the head, smiled at me, and left my room.

It is pretty hard for a dad to be mad at you when you are already crying really hard about another bad thing that has already happened, so I guess I was lucky about that.

MY CHIP-UP BAND-AID

He fixed everything for me.

EVERYTHING BACK TO NORMAL

At journal time I was looking out my window and watching Mrs. Witkins climb in her window again. Only this time it didn't seem so strange, because I was already kind of used to it and was expecting it. Right after Mrs. Witkins went in through the window, Mr. Hurley came out of his house with Oliver. I couldn't write about Mrs. Witkins again, so I decided to write about Oliver instead.

> *Oliver is a dog who lives right across the street from me. He lives with Mr. Hurley, who is his owner. Oliver does not like children, but Oliver does like to eat garbage he finds on the street. If Mr. Hurley let him, Oliver would probably eat all the garbage he found everywhere.*

Mimi and I did not look at each other through our windows before bed. I was sort of glad about that because I was super tired and I just wanted to go to sleep. This is not something that happens very often. I even let Chip-Up sleep next to me, and this time he was hardly even pointy or in the way at all.

MY MORNING

At breakfast time Mom said she was happy to see that Chip-Up was back to normal. And even Dad said good morning to him. Somehow, it was weird to have Mom and Dad being so nice to Chip-Up. I couldn't tell if that meant I was closer to getting a dog or further away from getting a dog. Parents are hard to understand. Plus, the awful part was that if I was closer to getting a dog, now I wouldn't even know what kind of dog to get. Emma had ruined everything.

DOG PARK

Since today was not a school day, Mimi, Max, Sammy, and I decided to go to the dog park first thing in the morning. Of course we left Chip-Up at home. We didn't want Emma to stick her teeth into him again. Max said that dog people like to walk their dogs first thing in the morning, so he was pretty sure that Bernie and his owner would be there. We were curious with wanting to know how Bernie's owner was going to help us.

On the way we saw Mr. Hurley walking back with Oliver. We all crossed the street so we wouldn't have to walk by them because of Oliver not being friendly to kids.

When we got to the park the dog people were all talking together in a circle and they did not look happy and smiley like usual. Mimi said that it was probably going to be bad news for us, because Bernie's owner was doing some pointing, and his pointing was in our direction.

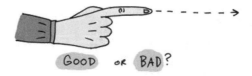

GOOD OR BAD?

WHAT WAS A SURPRISE

I was not wanting to have any more bad news in my life, so I said, "Let's just go home right now." I guess Mimi was thinking the same thing, because she said, "Okay." We were just starting to walk back when Max said, "Wait! They want us to come over. Look!"

We looked, and he was right: the dog people were moving their arms and hands in that come-over-here way. So we all had to walk over, even Sammy. "Sorry, kids," said Bernie's owner. "We've had some sad news. We were just talking about our friend August and his dog, Oliver."

I couldn't believe it. "Mr. Hurley's Oliver?" "That's right," said the man. "Well, I suppose you'd know him, what with you kids being so excited about dogs." "Well, we don't *know him* know him," said Sammy. "Oliver doesn't like kids." "Well, that may be true," said the man. "I don't know about that."

And then he told us the sad story of how Oliver was not eating his food anymore, and no matter what Mr. Hurley did, he could not get him to eat. And how Mr. Hurley was so worried that he was even making Oliver special meals of people food, but still that was not working either. Bernie's owner didn't say it, but I could tell that he was thinking that Oliver might even die!

Then he said, "Uh-oh, here comes trouble." And he was right. Trouble was running up to us at top speed. Emma jumped all over me like I was her fav-

orite person in the whole world and she had not only yesterday ripped the leg off of my special homemade pretend dog. It's surprisingly hard to be mad at a real dog when it is showing 100 percent love for you.

WHAT HAPPENED NEXT

Mr. Scott said that he was really sorry again, but this time it did not make me sad because Emma was licking my hand. Mr. Scott said that Emma was still young and she still had some things she needed to learn, and one of those things was to not chase skateboards. He said she loved to bite skateboard wheels and was probably so excited about the skateboard that she bit Chip-Up by accident and then unfortunately it just got worse from there.

I don't know why, but suddenly I was 100

percent forgiving her. Mimi did not feel the same, because when Emma came over to her, she just looked down at her and did not even give her a pat.

Mr. Scott didn't notice Mimi still being mad, because he said, "You kids are great. I want you to have these." Then he gave us each a free movie pass and some coupons for treats at the movie candy counter. Mimi couldn't be mad about that, and she wasn't, because now she was smiling too. I thought that was our big surprise, but then Bernie's owner said, "Do you kids want to hear my idea?" Of course you can't say no to something like that.

BERNIE'S OWNER'S IDEA

Bernie's owner's name was John. It was a lot easier to ask him questions about his idea once we knew what his name was. He told us what to call him after Max said, "Excuse me, Bernie's owner, do you mean you are going to pay us real money?" Max was asking that question because John wanted to know if we would walk his dog, Bernie, in the park on Mondays and Wednesdays after school. He said he had to work late those days for the next two weeks and would not be able to take Bernie out.

I couldn't believe that he was offering us a real job for money. And after he said he thought we were responsible and dependable, I totally knew we couldn't say no. John said that he lived across the street from the park so his house would not be hard for us to get to. Then the other dog people said that they would be there every day to help out if we had any problems. It was amazing. Suddenly we were in the dog club and we didn't even have to have our own dog.

PERFECT

On the way home I was so happy, I almost felt like if I tried it I would maybe even be able to fly. There was no way that Mom and Dad could say that I was not 100 percent responsible and dependable if I had a real job. Plus, the job was going to be amazing practice for when I got my own dog. It was so, so, so perfect! Mimi was happy too. She said she was going to save up all her money and buy something really great. She didn't know what it was going to be yet, but it was going to be fantastic. Max said that he was going to try to teach Bernie a new trick as a surprise for John when he got back. The only person who was not excited and not saying anything was Sammy.

Mom and Dad Have Ideas Too

Mom and Dad were even more surprised about the idea than we were, and they were full of questions, because it is not every day that you get to have the most perfect job in the whole world given to you as a surprise. It was lucky that John gave us a note to give to them, because after a while I got tired of answering all their questions about it.

Dad called John on the phone and made a plan for us all to meet the next day to go over what we would have to do on Monday. Mom let me break the rule about no phone calls after 8:00 p.m. so I could call Mimi, Max, and Sammy to tell them about it. Sammy was the only one who didn't sound excited. I told him he had to come but that he did not have to touch Bernie if he didn't want to. Even then he did not sound very happy or filled with joy.

WHAT I FORGOT ABOUT

I could hardly wait to work on my journal and write down all the things that had happened, because these were not things I wanted to forget about when I was old and couldn't remember anything. It was going to be fun to read all about my first job, that part I was sure of.

Today the most amazing thing ever happened and it was right when I wasn't expecting anything. John, who is one of the dog people, offered Mimi, Max, and Sammy and me a job to do dog walking. The two great things about this job are that we get paid and that it proves that I am responsible and dependable at 100 percent. Mom and Dad will get me a dog for sure!

I was just finished writing my journal when I heard Oliver barking. I couldn't see Mrs. Witkins anywhere, but then I saw Mr. Hurley walking down the steps with Oliver. The next thing I thought in my head was the perfect idea to help Mr. Hurley, and that is because my empathy power was just suddenly working.

My thought was "Poor Oliver, if only Mr. Hurley let him eat garbage. Then he wouldn't die from not eating." This may not sound like an amazing idea, but it really was, and it was an idea that could save Oliver's life.

I ran downstairs and made Dad come across the street with me so I could talk to Mr. Hurley. I was a little bit scared because I knew that Oliver didn't like me, and Mr. Hurley does not seem super friendly either. But when you are using your superpower,

you really can't worry too much about stuff
like that.

**MY EMPATHY SYMBOL IF I HAD A
SYMBOL LIKE SUPERMAN'S**

AN IDEA THAT COULD SAVE
A LIFE

I decided to say the idea really fast—that way
Dad and I wouldn't have to stand there, with
Oliver not liking me, for very long. So I said,
"Mr. Hurley, I think you should try hiding

Oliver's food outside on the street. That way when you take Oliver for a walk he will think it's garbage and eat it." Mr. Hurley was totally surprised! He asked me what my name was and then he said, "Grace, I don't know how you thought of it, but I think I'm going to have to try your idea right now. If you'll excuse me, I have some food to hide. Thank you so much for thinking of Oliver."

Dad and I walked back to the house and Dad was looking at me like he was surprised too and he said, "You know, when I was a kid I really liked dogs too." This was a great moment, because Dad's non–animal person outside shell was suddenly peeling off, and he didn't even notice it yet.

WHAT MR. HURLEY DID

I went upstairs and spied on Mr. Hurley from my window. I wanted to see if he was really going to do my idea. If I didn't know what he was doing, I would have said that Mr. Hurley looked like a big litterbug! He was walking around outside dropping food in little piles on the sidewalk and by the curb. After he was finished, he brought Oliver out. At first I couldn't tell what was happening or if it was working, but then when Mr. Hurley walked under one of the streetlights, I could see that he was smiling. Oliver was truly a garbage-loving dog. He even loved pretend garbage.

For the second night in a row I was super tired. Maybe all this thinking about real dogs was more work than just thinking about

Chip-Up. Poor Chip-Up—he didn't even get to go outside today. I was hoping Dad wouldn't notice that part.

JOHN'S HOUSE

John's house was right across the street from the park just like he said it was. Before we got there Dad told us that we had to be serious about our new job and that meant no fooling around. We all said yes, we knew that already, but I was still thinking that Bernie would probably like it better if there was at least a little bit of fooling around.

When we got there Dad and John did a lot of talking. At first it was sort of interesting stuff, but then it got really boring once Dad found out that John was a guy who knows a lot about trees and plants. Dad had all sorts of questions about how to fix up our yard, which I think looks perfectly fine just the way it is.

I was happy when John had the suggestion of us taking Bernie for a practice walk in the park while he and Dad watched from his front porch. Bernie is a good dog to practice on because he doesn't pull on his leash or want to chase squirrels or skateboard wheels. I was surprised, but I was liking Bernie a lot more than I thought I would.

Before I knew him, I would never have put his kind of dog, with little stubby legs, on my list of dogs I liked. But after spending time with him I could tell that if I had a dog like Bernie, I would love him very much. The most fun part was holding the leash, but I was good about it and let Max and Mimi have turns too. Sammy didn't want a turn at all.

WHO IS GOING TO DO IT

Everything was going perfectly, and then all
of a sudden Bernie pooped. Mimi said there
were poopy bags on the leash holder, so that
was lucky, but someone still had to pick it up.
I didn't want to do it because I didn't have my
rubber gloves with me. Mimi was holding
the leash so she said she couldn't do it. Max
said it was too stinky and he might throw up
if he got too close, so he couldn't do it. None
of us wanted to do it, and the worst thing
was that Dad and John were watching us. If

we didn't pick it up they would for sure take our dog walking job instantly and completely away from us.

Then Sammy said, "Boy, you are such a bunch of babies. I'll do it." And he pulled out the poopy bag and walked over and picked it up. It was like he was our surprise hero. Mimi even said a little "Yeah!"

WE DID IT

When we got back from the walk, Dad and John were still forever talking about trees. They said that we had done a great job, and this meant that we could keep our dog walking job, which was really good news. I couldn't tell if they knew that none of us wanted to pick up the poop. Hopefully they were too busy talking about trees to notice. Sammy had turned out to be a super-big helper on the dog team, even when he didn't like dogs!

John showed us where he hid his front door key so we could get into the house on Monday to pick up Bernie. And Dad made us all promise that we would not go poking through John's things, which we wouldn't have done anyway because we know it's not nice to be nosy like that. I almost couldn't wait for Monday to come.

On the way home Dad told us that John was a landscape architect. A regular architect is a person who draws designs so that people can make houses. A landscape architect draws where the grass and trees and rocks and bushes go. Dad said it was a very interesting job to have, but it didn't seem very exciting to me.

When we got back to my house we all sat together on the front lawn. Dad went inside but then he came back with a box of cookies. Max said, "Your dad is the greatest," which is mostly true, but he was not the greatest because of the cookies, because the cookies were not even from him.

There was a note on top of the box that said, "For Grace. Thank you, A. Hurley." Nobody saw the note but me, which was good because I didn't want to do a bunch of explaining about why Mr. Hurley was giving me a box of very delicious cookies to eat. Sometimes a person just gets tired of explaining stuff.

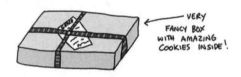

VERY
FANCY BOX
WITH AMAZING
COOKIES INSIDE!

WE ARE TRULY HAPPY

Max was super excited about our new job. He said when we had finished working for John we could make posters, and then we could do the dog walking job for other people too. It was so amazing to think that we were doing this great new thing. Even Sammy was excited.

I looked across the street to see if I could see Mr. Hurley. I kind of wanted him to see how much we were all liking his extra-delicious cookies. He wasn't there, but someone else was watching us, and I was 100 percent completely surprised that it was Grace L. She was sitting on the front steps of Mrs. Witkins's house, which is not a place I would ever think I would see her. Mimi saw me looking across the street, so she did too. Pretty soon we were all staring at Grace L., who was staring right back at us. I started to feel my guilty feeling again. It was the same guilty feeling that I had pretended to ignore when I was sitting with the other Graces and Grace L. was watching us. It was the kind of feeling that could make my tummy say it did not want anymore supertasty cookies.

"I wonder why Grace L. is sitting on Mrs. Witkins's steps," said Max. Then without thinking I said, "Let's find out," and I moved my arm and hand in that come-over-here way.

ONE LAST MYSTERY

Grace seemed a little shy at first but that was not for long. We had so many questions and such delicious cookies that she forgot about the being-shy part pretty fast. The reason we had so many questions is that she knew exactly why Mrs. Witkins had been sneaking into her basement window at night.

Grace L.'s mom is friends with Mrs. Witkins, which is why Grace L. was sitting on the outside steps. Mrs. Witkins was inside, showing Grace's mom a quilt she was making for her daughter Emily's birthday, which was in a couple of weeks. She wanted the quilt to be a surprise, so every night she left the house, saying she had to go to a meeting or shopping, but instead of going anywhere she snuck back inside through the window and worked on the quilt in the basement.

Grace said Mrs. Witkins had a huge bruise on her leg from falling through the window. She told us Mrs. Witkins had said, "It's not so easy to climb in and out of windows when you are old."

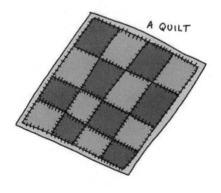

A QUILT

Sammy said he was a little disappointed that Mrs. Witkins was not a spy but just a sewing-loving person instead. Still, it was pretty cool that she was working so hard to make a nice surprise for Emily. Grace L. made us promise not to tell anyone about the quilt, because if Emily found out about it before her birthday, Mrs. Witkins would be 100 percent heartbroken. We all promised not to say anything, and I was pretty sure Sammy would keep the secret, because after Grace L. left he asked me what a quilt was.

MY LAST JOURNAL WRITING

I passed Dad on the way to my room and, feeling brave, I said, "Dad, can I have a dog?" He didn't say yes. He didn't say no. He said, "We'll see," which is total proof that his outside shell is breaking. If I weren't so tired I would flashlight Morse code Mimi all about it. Now all we have to do is pick out the kind of dog we want. This is not so easy, and it will probably take a long time, because dogs are a lot like people. There are a lot of M&M's out there. At first their outside seems like one thing, but then when you get to know them, you find out that underneath they are something else.

Mrs. Witkins was like a professional spy tonight. She disappeared into her basement window as quick as a flash, and that was because she had a new mysterious stool under the window to help her. Mr. Hurley dropped more litter around the neighborhood, and Oliver was happy about that. Chip-Up is sleeping on my bed again, and he looks just perfectly happy with his head on my pillow. Even though I have a job with a real dog, I'm going to keep him for a while, at least until I get my real dog, and I can just tell that's going to be happening pretty soon.

I had to write five sentences in the end because sometimes you can't say everything you need to say in just four sentences. I was sure that Miss Lois was not going to mind. She was a teacher and teachers all liked stuff like extra writing. Plus, it was nice to tell her how everything worked out—that way she wouldn't be wondering about it, because everyone likes to know how a story finishes at the end.

DOGS I WOULD NOT WANT AND WHY

Dear Miss Lois,

If you want to give me some extra marks for doing this extra part for my project then I will not be unhappy about that kind of thing happening.

SPANIEL (CLUMBER)

This kind of dog comes from England, which is a place I would like to visit, mostly because they speak English there and that would be helpful when you are on vacation. I read that these types of dogs drool and snore. This is not something I want to be happening at night when I am sleeping, especially if I let the dog sleep on my bed with me.

DOG HAS REALLY SAD EYES. ALWAYS LOOKS UNHAPPY

BEAGLE

This is another dog from England. It is a very cute dog, but it has a very powerful nose. Once it smells something it likes, it takes off and chases that smell, and even if you call it and call it, your dog will not come back. I do not want a running-away dog!

EXTRA-GOOD NOSE

PLOTT

This dog comes from the United States so you might think that it would be perfect for me, but that would not be true. It is the kind of dog that loves to hunt and chase bears. I hope to never have

TRAINED
BEAR HUNTER

bears near me, so this is not the kind of dog I am needing.

CHINESE CRESTED DOG

If there was an award for strangest-looking dog, this is totally the dog that would win. It's mostly funny-looking because it doesn't have hair on the main part of its body. It's the kind of dog that you have to dress in clothes or else it will get cold when you go outside. It

would probably be a good dog for
Valerie because she likes to make outfits.

KOMONDOR

This is a dog that looks like a giant
mop. You can't even see its face.

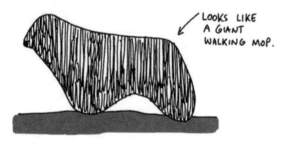

LOOKS LIKE
A GIANT
WALKING MOP.

This is the end of my report and most
of what I know about dogs that would
not be right for me.

WHAT GRACE WILL BE THINKING ABOUT IN HER NEXT BOOK